This Ladybird Book belongs to:

All children have a great ambition ... to read by themselves.

Through traditional and popular stories, each title in the **Read It Yourself** series introduces children to the most commonly used words in the English language (*Key Words*), plus additional words necessary to tell the story.
The additional words appearing in this book are listed below.

meadow, gate, closed, duck, swim, silly, argue, near, flies, safe, grandfather, wolf, swallows, gulp, inside, rope, ties, hunters, zoo, goes, played, flew, swam, took, wanted, sang, jumped, crept

Ladybird books are widely available, but in case of difficulty may be ordered by post or telephone from:

Ladybird Books – Cash Sales Department
Littlegate Road Paignton Devon TQ3 3BE
Telephone 0803 554761

A catalogue record for this book is available from the British Library

Published by Ladybird Books Ltd Loughborough Leicestershire UK
Ladybird Books Inc Auburn Maine 04210 USA

Ladybird

Peter and the Wolf

by Fran Hunia

illustrated by Kathie Layfield

Peter was at home
with his grandfather.

He wanted to go and play
in the big green meadow,
but the gate was closed.

There was a bird up in the tree
in the meadow.

The bird sang to Peter.
"All is quiet. Come on, Peter.
Come out into the meadow."

“Yes,” said Peter.
“Here I come.”

He opened the gate
and went out into the meadow.

Peter played with his hat
in the meadow.

The bird sang
up in the tree.

A duck came
into the meadow.
She looked at the water
and went for a swim.

The bird flew down
from the tree.

He said to the duck,
“You are a silly bird.
You can’t fly like I can.
See, I can fly like this.
Off I go, up over the trees.”

The duck said to the bird,
"You are a silly bird.
You can't swim.
Look, I can swim like this."
She swam fast
over the water.

They argued and argued,
the duck in the water
and the bird in the tree.

A cat came up.

He saw the duck
and the bird.
“I want to eat that bird,”
the cat said.

The duck in the water
and the bird in the tree
argued and argued.

They didn’t see the cat coming.

The cat crept near
to the duck and the bird.

Peter saw the cat.

"Look out!" he said.
"The cat will eat you."

The bird flew up
into the tree.

The duck swam away
on the water.

They were safe.

The cat looked up
at the bird
but could not get it.

Out came Peter's
grandfather.

"Come here, Peter,"
he said.
"You must come home
with me.
It's not safe out here
in the meadow.
A wolf may come
and get you."

Grandfather took Peter
away from the meadow.

They went home
and Grandfather closed
the gate.

Peter was safe by the house.

As soon as Peter had gone, a wolf came out of the trees and into the meadow.

He saw the cat, the duck and the bird.

He wanted to eat them.

The cat saw the wolf
and jumped quickly
up into the tree
with the bird.

Now they were safe
from the wolf.
He could not eat them.

The duck saw the wolf.

She jumped out of the water
and ran away fast.

The wolf ran after the duck.
He got her
and swallowed her down
in one gulp.

The cat and the bird
were up in the tree.

They were safe.

The wolf went
round and round the tree
but he could not get up
to eat them.

Peter looked out
into the meadow and saw
the wolf.

Peter went inside
to get a rope.
He took the rope
up into the tree.

He was going
to get the wolf.

He would not let it eat
the bird or the cat.

When Peter got up
to the bird, he said,
“Fly round the wolf,
please, but don’t
let him eat you.
I want to get him
with this rope.”

The bird flew down
from the tree.

The bird flew
round and round the wolf.

Peter tied the rope
to the tree.

He let the rope down.

Peter got the wolf
with his rope.

The wolf jumped up and down,
but he could not get away.

Some hunters came.
They were looking for the wolf.
"Look," said Peter.
"The wolf is over there
by the tree.
He can't get away.
Please help me
to take him
to the zoo."

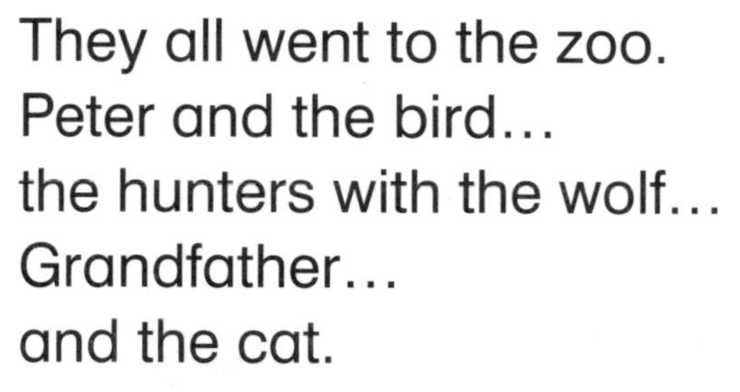

They all went to the zoo.
Peter and the bird...
the hunters with the wolf...
Grandfather...
and the cat.

Now that the wolf
was safe in the zoo,
Peter could play
out in the meadow.

All was quiet once more.